Edward Ca

The Art of Pluck.: Being a Treatise After The Fashion of Aristotle; Writ For The Use of Students In University

outlook

Edward Caswall

The Art of Pluck.: Being a Treatise After The Fashion of Aristotle; Writ For The Use of Students In University

Reprint of the original, first published in 1843.

1st Edition 2024 | ISBN: 978-3-38512-373-1

Verlag (Publisher): Outlook Verlag GmbH, Zeilweg 44, 60439 Frankfurt, Deutschland
Vertretungsberechtigt (Authorized to represent): E. Roepke, Zeilweg 44, 60439 Frankfurt, Deutschland
Druck (Print): Books on Demand GmbH, In de Tarpen 42, 22848 Norderstedt, Deutschland

THE ART OF PLUCK.

BEING

A TREATISE

AFTER THE

FASHION OF ARISTOTLE;

WRIT FOR THE USE OF STUDENTS IN THE UNIVERSITIES.

TO WHICH IS ADDED,

FRAGMENTS FROM THE EXAMINATION PAPERS.

Ridiculum acri
Fortius ac melius magnas plerumque secat res.　　HOR. SAT.

Πᾶσα τέχνη καὶ πᾶσα μέθοδος ἀγαθοῦ
τινος ἐφίεσθαι δοκεῖ.　　ARIST. Eth. Lib. 1.

Thus have I described and opened those peccant humours which have given impediment to the proficience of learning, wherein if I have been too plain, it must be remembered "Fidelia vulnera amantis, sed dolosa oscula malignantis."
BACON'S ADVANCEMENT OF LEARNING.

BY

SCRIBLERUS REDIVIVUS.

Eighth Edition.

OXFORD:

PRINTED AND PUBLISHED BY J. VINCENT.

1843.

TO THE REV. HENRY FORMBY.

My dear Formby,

It was a curiously mixed feeling with which I heard the other day from the Publisher of this little work, that a new edition of it was about to appear.

You, who were among my contemporaries at Brasenose when it first came out, can doubtless still remember the sudden popularity which it obtained, not only amongst the Undergraduates of that day, but even with the more sober Bachelors, and in part too at the very High Tables. By all which surprised and delighted as I was at the time, I little expected that The Art would ever survive the term, much less continue to this period.

Generations which in the great world are reckoned three to a century, are in the Universities of but a brief date. There every term beholds as it were a fresh race ushered in, and an old race depart; an evanescent population of gownsmen grows up, flourishes, and dies away with marvellous rapidity. And, as Lucretius has it,

> Augescunt aliæ gentes, aliæ minuuntur:
> Inde brevi spatio mutantur sæcla animantum,
> Et, quasi cursores vitaï lampada tradunt.

Hence it comes to pass, that on looking back upon

the origin of this little book, and perceiving through
how many terms it has survived, I seem to behold it
already invested as-it were with an ephemeral antiquity; and, on comparing the present with the past,
am hardly able to realize to myself that I was the
actual author of it; and reasons indeed there are,
why in one respect I might wish this were truly the
case.

Tempora mutantur nos et mutamur in illis.

You who have been with me, and known my private
sentiments during the changeful interval which has
elapsed since our Undergraduate days, will bear me
witness how from year to year, with increasing
thoughtfulness, I have learnt more and more to regret
the introduction both into this book, and that called
the Examination Papers, of certain passages, con-
taining sentences from Holy Scripture. I refer particularly to certain anecdotes, introduced under the
head of Answers in Divinity, the profaneness of which,
to my shame be it said, I did not at the time perceive.
Not that I actually invented any one of these, for
indeed I did but borrow them from the current anecdotes of the day; nevertheless, even with this allowance, I have in later years come to perceive, that
in those times, in the vanity of my mind, and the
desire of making my Art as effective as possible, I
committed no small sin, doing thoughtlessly what lay
in my power towards investing certain passages of the
Divine Word with ridiculous associations.

If for no other cause, yet for this, that this confession of mine may continue to bear witness against me
in this respect, I earnestly hope that this book may
last. And I here solemnly affirm, that whatever were
the pleasures of gratified vanity, which as an Undergraduate I experienced from the rapid popularity
which this pamphlet acquired in both Universities,
they have been more than counterbalanced in later
years by the consideration of the dishonour therein
done by me to the Word of God, and the great injury
committed against the Church of Christ, the witness
and keeper of that Word. And this I here record,
not only as my own humble confession, that as the sin
was public, so may also be the acknowledgment of
it; but as a warning to those Undergraduates who
shall hereafter read this work, lest they should, in the
heyday of youthful ambition, fall into the same or a
similar error.

Alas! how true is it, "Nescit vox missa reverti;"
and again, "Volat irrevocabile verbum;" and again,
"By thy words thou shalt be justified, and by thy
words thou shalt be condemned!"

In respect to the work as now published, that is to
say, with the omission of those particular anecdotes,
my honest conviction is, that it exhibits, in a plain
and conclusive view, the essential absurdity and folly
of that miserable course which by too many young
men of our Universities is so studiously pursued,
as though it were the end of their residence. Which,

if it be absurd in the sight of man, and by the dictates of common sense, (which is all that this treatise professes to shew,) let every person reflect for himself, what such a waste of time, opportunities, and energies must appear in the sight of God, and when judged by his Holy Law.

To you, my dear friend, whose office, like my own, is now something more than to ridicule vice as absurd, I dedicate these pages; in the humble hope that nothing remains in them which need cause you shame on my account. And I here conclude, with expressing my high veneration for the authorities and discipline of both Universities, and my trust that nothing in this book will ever be construed as casting any slight upon them. Did I think so, I would long since have done my best, at any expense, to put a stop to the present publication of it, as I did two years back in respect to the Examination Papers; a few extracts from which is all that I judge proper to be appended to this edition.

Ever, my dear FORMBY,

Faithfully yours,

EDWARD CASWALL.

Vicarage House, Stratford Sub-Castle,
Feb. 3rd, 1843.

CONTENTS.

BOOK III.

ADVERTISEMENT TO THE THIRD EDITION.

Whereas in my former Prefaces I addressed the students of Oxford, so here I desire further the Students of Cambridge to understand, that this book may be turned to their own account also, if they will be pleased to consider not so much the form of it as the matter. Thus as in other studies there hath ever been a generous rivalry between Cambridge and Oxford, so let it be hoped that in pursuit of Plucks also, these two Universities shall each, by aid of this book, mutually strive to supersede the other, that there be no disparity left betwixt them.

PREFACE.

THIS Preface divideth itself into three parts; whereof first, the usefulness of the art;* second, the history of it; third, the derivation of the word. To begin then with each in its own order. First, for the usefulness of the art, which indeed wanteth no proof for persons unprejudiced; but whereas the generality is not of this sort, I think best to say thus much upon it. For it is a thing not to be denied, that every art is good in proportion as it assisteth in producing some end, whereat mankind do aim in common. Now of this kind is the Art of Pluck; for upon looking about this University, who doth not see that to be plucked is an end pursued by many persons, yea and these persons, such as from their age cannot be said not to have judgment? To these then and the like, this art teacheth an easy way to this their end, by a collection of subtle rules long practised at random, but till now never brought down to the axioms of true philosophy. Whereat let people wonder, if they please; yet was the same the case with all arts at the beginning, as hath been acutely said of Logic. Let so much have been said about the usefulness of this art, which indeed deserveth rather the name of a science, inasmuch as it not only serveth for an instrument, but likewise discusseth, as will be seen, the principles of Pluck. Nevertheless as it is still in its infant condition, content we with the term Art, and so to proceed with what cometh next in order.

Now it may seem strange to the learned, that whereas I have said the Art of Pluck is new, I come next to a history of it.† For history is of things past, and therefore old for the most part. Yet though the art be new, true it is, the thing itself hath existed

* Vide Aristot. Rhet. lib. i. cap. 1.
† Vide Whately's Introduction to the Art of Logic.

a long while, yea, even from the days of Cheops, who was the
first to found a college.   Niebuhr * indeed hath it, that the
custom of Pluck was brought to this college twenty-five years
after the death of Cheops, in the Egyptian month Pilko, by an
Ethiopian priest surnamed Hushmug: against which disputeth
Müller in four volumes, that the name was not Hushmug but
Hugmush.   Yet after all this disputation, still do I keep to
my old opinion, for if Cheops builded a college, needs must he
have founded Plucks at the same time; since in our own days
no college existeth a year without a Pluck; whence it followeth
that a college without Plucks is no real college.   Yet was the
college of Cheops a real college, and therefore needs must it have
had Plucks.   But to proceed with the history.   It seemeth, that
after the days of Cheops, Plucks spread abroad exceedingly, till
they reached even to the Pelasgi, by which people were they
carried into Greece.   For that the descent of the Pelasgi was
about this time, Herodotus doth amply testify; nor is it to be
doubted that they brought wisdom into Greece, and therefore
Plucks.   Yet at this time were Plucks of but a simple kind,
without distinction of Little-go and Great-go, which waited for
the wisdom of later ages.   But as science grew, and books were
writ, so did Plucks increase in the gradual progression of things.
For it is a truth not yet noted by philosophy, that as the circle of
knowledge extendeth, so also extendeth the circle of not knowing,
whereby was Euclid of great use to Plucks even in that age.
Thus may it be said that Plucks went on hand in hand with wisdom in all Greece, but most in Athens, where was most wisdom,
till at the last, after the conquest of Corinth, they were carried to
Rome, there to flourish till the dark ages.   Yet was Athens not
deprived of Plucks by this conquest: for being the University of
the world, thither did flock all such as loved wisdom; yea of
Cicero himself it is said, that he was plucked twice by reason
that he could not pass the asses' bridge.   As for the dark ages,

* Vide the Frankfort edition, which was published in 1829.

Plucks had been lost to the world in those times, but for the monasteries; wherein were they preserved, together with other wise institutions, till these modern times, in the which by slow degrees our Universities have brought them to perfection. For now, beside the new distinction of Little-go and Great-go, a man may be plucked for different kinds of ignorance, each of which possesseth its own discriminations, to be detailed hereafter.

For the derivation of the word Pluck, to which I now proceed, it hath ever been a matter of great dubiousness. One person of no small wisdom saith, that a man is said to be plucked by contraries; that is to say, because at such a time he loseth all Pluck. The which argument I would allow to be true, but that the premiss is false. For many there be, who by being plucked grow yet more plucky, as was the case with Sir Giles C******* of ******; which gentleman, after being plucked, gave a party the same evening, declaring that he minded it not at all, yea rather gloried therein. So falleth this first argument to the ground, to which followeth this other. For indeed it was an ancient custom in Oxford, whereof there be still remains, that when a man was turned back in his examination, a person should pluck the Proctor's gown, whereby as he proceeded to give him a degree he was stopped in the midst. Hence, as the antiquarians do say, it came to pass that the man´so losing his degree, was said to be plucked. Yet in this argument also is there no small flaw, which the love of truth compelleth me to make plain, after the example of Aristotle, albeit against my inclination. For verily it is the man who is said to be plucked now-a-days, not the Proctor; the which thing differeth not a little. Many other arguments there be on this matter, but I proceed to my own opinion, as being what seemeth to me the best. For, first, what meaneth Pluck? Doth it not signify, to lose one's feathers? the which is suffered metaphorically by every man turned in his examination. To me then it seemeth that a man is said to be plucked from analogy to a bird; but what that bird be, whether big or little, land or water bird, I pretend not to say. The like analogy, as a further proof, is to be noted betwixt a man and a bird, not only at his Pluck, but also before and after; for he is said to be crammed first, and to have been well roasted by the examiner afterward.

And now to conclude this Preface with one thing more in praise of this Art of Pluck; let it be known that it shareth with Analytics and Rhetoric alone of all arts, it being an art of contraries. For as it teacheth a person how best to be plucked, so also by the addition of *not* to each rule, it teacheth a person how not to be plucked, if there be any such. But on this and the rest enough hath been said for Preface, so proceed we to the Art with all attention.

PREFACE TO THE SECOND EDITION.

Learned reader, Aristotle saith that "time is a fellow-worker with philosophers in producing the perfection of science," the which thing is to be observed not a little in mine own case. For it being six days since this Art was first published to the world, in that time have many new lights appeared to me concerning it. For being at present concealed, I do hear myself praised and blamed daily before my face. Nay, mine own friends, at such times as they have nothing else to talk about, tell me their opinion of this new Art, giving likewise the name of the author, with no small assurance. In this second Preface, I would have thee understand that I put into thy hands the same Art indeed as before, but with certain additions, especially from the examinations just finished. These additions, if thou art really and truly studious in ignorance and idleness, thou wilt find out of thyself in the reading of this book; of which let me say to its praise, that there hath been no other book published in Oxford in the reading whereof thou mightest more easily go to sleep, and so be idle, and get plucked accordingly. Which last wishing thee, as many times over as thou desirest, I remain thy friend and fellow-gownsman,

SCRIBLERUS REDIVIVUS.

Nov. 13th, 1835.

BOOK I.

CHAP. I.

A Division of the Treatise.

LET the Art[a] of Pluck be that art which teacheth how most thoroughly to be plucked, the easiest way, in the shortest time, under a case the most difficult.[b] For truly, it is an easy task to be plucked, for one ignorant altogether of things; but the fine thing is, for one who cometh from school well laden with knowledge, so to demean himself as to come to be plucked in the end, and that in a short time, not for one ignorance only, as of Euclid, but for many, the which thing teacheth this Art.

Now of "Plucks" there be in this age two kinds: firstly, the Pluck in Little-go; secondly, the Pluck in Great-go. But as Aristotle in his Poetics hath thought fit to discuss chiefly Tragedy, by reason that it embraceth within itself all questions pertaining to the other sorts of poesy, so let us also in this art of Pluck discuss the Great-go Pluck for

---

[a] Vide Rhet. lib. i. cap. 2.

[b] Let it not be understood from this, that this art concerneth theory only, and not practice; for, as Aristotle saith in his Poetics, τὸ τέλος πρᾶξις τίς ἐστιν; and again in his Ethics, lib. ii. cap. 2. οὐ γὰρ ἵν᾽ εἰδῶμεν τί ἐστιν ἡ ἀρετὴ, σκεπτόμεθα· ἀλλ᾽ ἵν᾽ ἀγαθοὶ γενόμεθα. Subject of the Essay, Mich. Term.

the most part, bringing in at the end such distinctions between the two as shall seem fit. For indeed doth not Great-go, besides what it hath of its own, include all the appurtenances of Littlego, such as Euclid, Logic, Horace, Virgil, and all else ?

This thing then being settled, it remaineth to discuss the Great-go Pluck; which discussion divideth itself into two parts, as followeth. For a man is plucked, firstly, by the preparation of ignorance which he maketh thereto before his Examination; secondly, by the way he carrieth himself at his Examination. Now these two things are different, and beside them there is nothing else. Let then be discussed in the first place the preparation of ignorance before Examination.

CHAP. II.

A still further Division.

BUT this preparation likewise divideth itself into two kinds, whereof one is a preparation direct, the other a preparation indirect. The first includeth such methods of Construing, of Parsing, of Logic, of Euclid, of Divinity, and the rest, as be most fit to gain a full Pluck; the second includeth all kinds of Idleness, whereby the mind is put into the best channel of ignorance for the same.

CHAP. III.

Concerning Construing.

To begin then with the preparation direct, whereof first cometh Construing. Now construing is divided into two kinds: first, to construe Latin; second, to construe Greek; of which each taketh three subdivisions: first, to construe well; second, to construe right; third, to construe wrong. But of these three the last alone serveth to Pluck, being verily an easy thing to do simply; as, for example sake, to construe *amo*, "thou lovest." Yet in a complexity of words where there be many ways of construing wrong, yea truly a difficult thing it is to construe the wrongest way; the which thing he who doth best, hath best likelihood of gaining a full Pluck. Whereof let the following be examples for imitation.

As first, since *vices* meaneth shiftings and changings, to construe *mutat terra vices*, "the earth changeth her shift." So from the same author, *horridus aper*, "a horrid . bore." And whereas Livy hath the following sentence, *Hannibal Alpes transivit summa diligentia*, which meaneth, "Hannibal passed over the Alps as fast as he could;" so let him who desireth a Pluck, departing from this method, construe it thus, "Hannibal passed over the Alps on the top of a diligence." Likewise *Ite Capellæ*, "Go it you cripples."

Nostri pugnabant rari, "Our men fought uncommon." *Ex tu Brute*, "You brute you." *Mala duces avi domum*, "Thou bringest apples to the house of thy grandfather." So much for Latin. Then for Greek as followeth: " Ὤμοι πέπληγμαι, Æsch. Agam. 1314. "Oh dear! I'm blowed." Αἰτήσοντες γῆν καὶ ὕδωρ, "To ask for gin and water." Δηναιαὶ κόραι, Prom. 819. "Old maids." Ἀμφὶ δ' ὀφθάλμοις φόβος, Persæ. "My eyes! what a funk I'm in." From which examples is seen how, first, simple words which cannot be construed wrong, so far as grammar concerneth, may yet be turned to a wrong meaning by fit attention: how, secondly, a complex sentence so turned to a wrong meaning, may yet be further improved in wrongness by bad grammar: as happened with Mr. Thomas T*** of *****, who, when he had construed *Hannibal Alpes transivit summa diligentia*, "Hannibal passed over the Alps on the top of a diligence," was straightway reproved by the examiner, as having construed wrong: whereon he yet improved the wrongness by bad grammar, construing thus; "the Alps passed over Hannibal on the top of a diligence:" and again, by yet worse grammar, "a diligence passed over Hannibal on the top of the Alps." So much for good construing; which requireth further, that in place of originals thou read translations, especially such as be of a free kind.

CHAP. IV.

Concerning Parsing.

As for Parsing, which cometh next in order, it requireth but little to say upon it. Only let each remember, where he .can, for masculine to say feminine; for singular, plural; for nominative, accusative; and so on through all the divers ramifications of nouns adjective and substantive. For verbs, let him not omit to put active for passive, present for past, and future for present; whereby he will gain a Pluck in good style. Yet to this end doth Greek offer more facility than Latin, for that it hath a middle voice, which the Latin hath not, or but a little. Likewise it hath *paulo post futurums,* whereby boys at school do get floggings many, insomuch that at one time it was meditated by the learned to dismiss *paulo post futurums* altogether; yet still do they exist, for the sake of making an easy way to Plucks. Now to proceed.

CHAP. V.

Concerning Logic.

LOGIC is defined to be that instrumental art which helpeth a man to be plucked in his Little-go and Great-go by aid of his reason. For verily as the right use of Logic doth give an acuteness and readiness to the intellect, so doth the wrong use thereof mystify the mind and lead to Pluck.

Among good examples of Logic take the following. For definition, as of Oxford nominally, " a place where oxen do ford through;" accidently, " a learned society;" essentially, " a place where are many Plucks." For division, as of " a plum cake into raisins and suet;" of " a kingdom into Tories and Whigs." For proposition, as when it was "proposed to admit Dissenters," which proposition, as was indeed affirmative at the first, but became negative afterward. For the mood of a proposition, as when that proposition being so negatived did put the Dissenters in an " ill mood." For conversion, " some wives love their husbands," converted to, " all husbands love their wives."— " Nothing is better than a good conscience," converted to, " a good conscience is better than nothing."—" I saw two cats fighting on the leads," converted to, " I saw two dogs fighting in the street." As for syllogism, which in cases of Pluck is called " sillygism," it hath divers kinds, whereof let suffice one instance, as

All reading men are animals.
Some animals (that is to say, pigs) are learned
Therefore is it not to be denied that some reading men
   are pigs.

CHAP. VI.

Concerning Euclid.

OF Euclid is but little to be said, save that for
Pluck it is best to be learned by rote and not by
understanding. Also, to the same end, it is a
good thing to take for granted such problems as
be difficult to learn. Wherefore let thy Euclid be
bought second-hand, for so shall two advantages
accrue to thee; inasmuch as, firstly, thou shalt
know by the thumbing which be the hard problems, and so avoid them; secondly, of that same
thumbing shalt thou have the glory when thou
shewest the book to thy governor.

CHAP. VII.

Concerning History.

OF History useful to Pluck are there four di-
visions, for the most part; that is to say, Herodotus, Thucydides, Livy, and Tacitus; whereof Herodotus produceth Plucks in proportion 40, Thucydides 39, Livy 53, and Tacitus 44; whence
it appeareth that Thucydides produceth fewest
Plucks, and Livy most. Now the reason of this
is, that Thucydides being difficult is most studied,
but Livy being easy is studied but a little, being
read for the most part (that is to say, the second

decade) in an analysis. In the reading of History for Pluck, let each be mindful to consider of chronology as of a separate thing, not to be mixed up with history; for indeed history is of things, but chronology of times. Therefore let him be careful either, first, not to read chronology at all; or, secondly, to read it in such a way as for it to have no congruity with history. For example, let him put Pericles after Cicero, and Virgil before Thucydides; this being the true way, which in geography also is to be observed. For as Sparta is commonly said to be in the Peloponnesus, and Ephesus in Asia Minor, so let him who aimeth at a good Pluck put Sparta boldly into the Baltic, and Ephesus among the "Silly" islands. Also, let each consider this general rule, that in proportion as a book is more difficult, so if it be the less studied it will produce more Plucks. Likewise this- other, that if a person remember not one particular event of history, the first that he calleth to mind will do in its stead. The same for names also, as to put for Alcibiades, Heliogabalus; for Julius Cæsar, The king of the Cannibal Islands.

CHAP. VIII.

Concerning Divinity.

NEXT cometh a discussion of the kind of Divinity needful for Pluck, whereto let the rules following suffice.

First, Let a man make himself master of many and divers answers in Divinity from Watts's Scripture History; which let be done in the morning before examination, so when his examination cometh, let him put in one of the answers that first riseth to his memory, not minding the question at all. For examples in Divinity good for plucking take the following. Where was Galilee? Ans. In the middle of Samaria.—Who were the Publicans? Ans. Pharisees.—What do you mean by the Pentateuch? Ans. The ten commandments.

Secondly, It is best not to read the Bible; yet if a man do, let him read forty chapters a day at the least.

Thirdly, Let a man be careful not to listen to what is read each day in chapel, for thereby he will escape much knowledge of divinity. For which reason let him at chapel read a novel instead of the Prayer Book.

Fourthly and lastly, Let a man consider of divinity that it is an easy thing, and to be got up in half a day; so will he come to be plucked more surely: for he will ever put it off to the last, as in human life is the custom also.

CHAP. IX.

Concerning Sciences.

SCIENCES are useful to Pluck but seldom, for indeed few persons do take up sciences for a Pluck,

save as did Mr. Andrew D*****, who being con-
scious of knowing nothing, nevertheless went up
for a first class, hoping cunningly so to pass.
However, he succeeded not, but was plucked yet
the more. , Therefore of sciences I have but little
to say,^c save that it is best for Pluck to read no
more than an analysis of them in English the
night before.

CHAP. X.

Concerning the composition of Latin and Greek.

FOR writing Latin and Greek, consider well the
rules for construing and parsing, writ above,
which will suffice for the most part.   Yet must it
not be omitted, that useful also are letters wrigged
and tortuous, whereby the examiner is puzzled in
the reading; wherefore further do I recommend a
bad pen, that spurteth the ink: and mind, moreover, that as soon as possible after coming to
College thou lose the penknife which thy aunt
gave thee.

   Among examples of Latin composition good for
plucking, take these following: *a man of a good
constitution,* "homo bonæ reipublicæ;" *they came*

---

   ^c It requireth a full and perfect ignorance of philosophy, both
ancient and modern, to understand the sciences in a way useful
towards Pluck.   Nevertheless many persons in Oxford do attain
to this every year; for which they are highly to be praised.

down at a quick rate, "celeri rate descenderunt; *a woman of good carriage,* "mulier boni vehiculi;" *Theodosius was the younger son of a decayed family,* "Theodosius erat junior filius corrosæ familiæ; *it is well to punish tyrants,* "bene est ad puniendum tyrannorum." Also in spelling, as to spell Horatius, *Horatious,* and the like.

These examples are enough for diligent learners. As for examples in Greek, they are not needful; for he that writeth bad Latin can also write bad Greek, if it be necessary; albeit he that writeth good Latin, cannot for that reason write good Greek also.

CHAP. XI.

Concerning Poesy.

As for Poesy, it compriseth many books useful to Pluck, whereof are most in use, Virgil, Horace, Juvenal, and Euripides. Now these poets, when they wrote, knew not the high use to which their books would be put. Yet nevertheless have they by intuition writ many things easy to be mistaken, and therefore useful to Pluck. Nay, indeed, where they have writ in a clear manner, still it is possible to construe them wrong, as hath been before shewn. Therefore let every one in learning them, take care out of many bad meanings to choose the worst. Here also, to conclude, do I give this

further rule for poesy and prose, which deserveth
no small attention; that is to say, to construe
prose as if it were poesy, and poesy as if it were
prose.

BOOK II.

CHAP. I.

Concerning Idleness.

THUS much for the preparation direct for pluck-ing; to which followeth next in order the prepara-tion indirect, that is to say, Idleness. Whereof do both require much care and attention, but most of all the latter. For indeed it is a hard thing to be idle for a continuance, and requireth study; the which thing teacheth Virgil, when he saith *studiis otii :* the which also is to be seen in the idle per-sons themselves, who for the most part do seem weary and way-begone; shewing how hard a thing it is, and what trouble it taketh to be well plucked.

CHAP. II.

The Idleness of Smoking.

OF Idlenesses there be many; among which first cometh the idleness of smoking. Smoking is defined to be the sucking in of smoke at one part of the mouth, and the ejection thereof at another part. Yet is there a difference (as Ari-stotle saith of justice) between a smoker and him who smoketh; for the first hath the habit of

smoking, which the last hath not yet. Of smoking
there be two grand kinds : first, with a cigar ; second, with a pipe. Whereof the smoking with a
cigar is divided into two kinds : first, with a cigar
of paper, as at school ;[d] second, with a cigar of
tobacco, as at college : whence cometh a still
further subdivision of the first into white paper
or brown paper, according to quality; thin or thick,
according to substance ; long or short, according
to quantity. In like manner also is subdivided
the cigar of tobacco, according to its different
kinds. As for the other grand division, the
smoking with a pipe divideth itself into two kinds :
first, with a common clay; second, with a German
pipe. Whereof the first is subdivided into the
straight pipe ; the twisted pipe of modern fashion ;
the pipe with a plain bowl; the pipe with a
flowery bowl; the pipe with red sealing-wax at
the end, the pipe with black sealing-wax, the pipe
with no sealing-wax ; the pipe with resin ; the pipe
full length ; the pipe broken short, (as is the pipe
of a coal-heaver,) and so on. For the German
pipe, it admitteth of no division save division of
age, seeing that the best German pipe is that

[d] Likewise on the continent do they smoke cigars of paper,
with this difference, that there they put tobacco inside, but at
school the cigar is of paper wholly: whence it is seen how wrong
was Mr. H * * *, who said of this book that it was written by
a man who knew not the noble science of smoking, for that he
spoke of "*paper* cigars."

which hath been longest smoked; for which
reason it is in use with a certain tobacconist of
High-street to employ, on direction, two boys for
smoking new pipes into old: and thus much for
the instrument wherewith smoking is done.

As for the manner of smoking, it is of divers
kinds. Some do smoke sitting, some walking, and
some standing. For sitting, a man may smoke,
first, in his own rooms; second, in another man's
rooms; each of which admitteth the subdivision
following. For it is possible to smoke at the fire:
which may be done, first, with legs over the grate;
second, with legs on the grate; third, with legs
under the grate. And it is possible to smoke at
table: which may be done, first, at breakfast; second, at luncheon; third at wine; fourth, at tea;
fifth, at supper; sixth, in bed; which last is most
practised.

For walking, a man may smoke walking in his
rooms, walking on the leads, walking in Quad,
walking to lecture, walking to chapel, walking in
High-street, walking to the river. For standing,
a man may smoke standing at the Porter's lodge,
standing on his legs, standing on his head, standing in another man's way, standing in his own
way.

Now all these instruments and manners of
smoking are useful to Pluck; but as to which
produceth most idleness, and therefore most Pluck,
it is hard to say; for every one differeth in his

adaptation to things external. Yet in the abstract
is standing more idle than walking, and therefore
to be preferred; as likewise is sitting more idle
than standing. Also in the abstract, to smoke
with a German pipe hath in it more of laziness
than to smoke with a cigar; for why? He who
smoketh with a cigar hath need to reach his hand
for another when the first is smoked; but he that
useth a German pipe may sit a long while, for
that it lasteth longer. Therefore it is found in
the records of Oxford, that in the year 1833, of
those that used German pipes were plucked 72,
but of those that used cigars only 53. Whence
for the most part do I recommend German pipes,
as being the better way of prosecuting idleness
with vigour.

CHAP. III.

The Idleness of Love.

NEXT cometh the idleness of Love, which leadeth
to no few Plucks. For he that is in love,[e] albeit
his dictionary lie open before him, thinketh not of
study. He walketh backward and forward in his
rooms; he turneth his back to the fire, lifting up
his coat-tail; he looketh out of the window,
wishing to be a bird; he openeth the most secret
part of his desk for a lock of hair; and so passeth

[e] Vide Rhet. lib. i. cap. 5.

his time, thinking thereon till his Little-go or Great-go cometh unawares.

Of love are there divers kinds, according to the person loved; wherefore it followeth to consider, what sort of lady produceth the love most likely to cause Pluck.

Now ladies may be considered in three ways: first, as to substance; second, as to quality; third, as to relation.

Under category of substance cometh the rich lady, the fat lady, the tall lady, the heavy lady, the plump lady, together with the contraries thereto, as the poor lady, the thin lady, the short lady, the light lady, the skinny lady.[f]

For quality, it is of two kinds: first, of person; second, of mind. Under the first cometh the round-faced lady, the long-faced lady, the wide-faced lady, the Roman-nosed lady, the red-haired lady, the gooseberry-eyed lady, with their opposites. Under the second cometh the amiable lady, the romantic lady, the quick lady, the sensible lady, the flirting lady, all these with their opposites.

Lastly; under category of relation cometh, first, the lady without relations, the widow, the ward in Chancery, the lady without brothers, the lady with first cousins, the lady with first cousins once re-

[f] Thus Aristotle hath, Rhet. lib. i. cap. 5, θηλειῶν ἀρετὴ σώματος μέγεθος, κ.τ.λ. See also, for what followeth, his doctrine concerning noses.

moved, and so on. Secondly, relation to age; as
the young lady, the middle-aged lady, the old
maid, the lady with teeth, the lady without teeth,
the lady that useth paint, the little girl, the big
girl, the old lady, and so on.

Wherefore in considering the lady most likely
to produce Pluck, there being three things con-
cerned,—first, substance; second, quality; third,
relation,—it followeth that the lady to be chosen,
is she who hath the best in each. As in substance, the rich lady is best; in quality of person,
the Roman-nosed lady; in quality of mind, the
romantic lady; in relation, the lady without brothers, and the young lady. Yet is it after all a
matter uncertain which lady produceth most love,
and therefore most idleness in each particular
person. For sometimes a young man falleth in
love with an old lady having money, as happened
with Mr. Andrew D****, who was plucked at
Little-go in 1827; and sometimes a handsome
man falleth in love with a gooseberry-eyed, fat,
poor, red-haired lady, if she be amiable; of which
last however hath been but one example in Oxford. Therefore, as I said, is the matter of love
an uncertain thing; yet from what hath been here
writ concerning it, may one nevertheless learn
something of it at the least, as regardeth Pluck
in the abstract. And now to proceed to other
idlenesses.

CHAP. IV.

Of the Idleness of Novels.

NEXT to the idleness of love cometh the idleness of reading novels, inasmuch as they concern love for the most part. Now novels are to be considered, first, as to the most fitting time for reading them; second, in respect of their kinds. For time: the best time to read a novel is just before thy examination, for thereby the mind is diverted from study, and so produceth Pluck; also let thy reading be at night for the most part, for in day time thou hast other idlenesses busying thee. As for the kinds of novels, they be divers : as, first, in respect of age, the novel well thumbed, the novel that is sticky, the old novel new bound, the novel whence the preface is torn, the novel whence the conclusion is torn : second, in respect of subject, as the novel that hath many love scenes, which is called by Mr. Bulwer, in speaking of his own novels, the novel philosophical; the novel maritime, which treateth of sailors' oaths; the novel fashionable, which bringeth high life down stairs, · and discusseth ladies' maids ; the novel of real life, which treateth of elopements; the novel religious, wherein pretty Protestants do convert Roman Catholics : third, in respect of manner, as the novel which sendeth asleep, the novel which letteth go to sleep, the novel which keepeth

asleep. Now all these sorts are useful to Pluck;
wherefore let them be read abundantly, and without ceasing, so that the boy who carrieth the
novels be even tired thereby: nor let it be forgot
to scribble notes on the leaves with thy philosophical opinion of things; as of the author, that he
is "a great ass;" of the book, that it is "badly
written, and very absurd throughout;" and of
certain expressions, that "there is no such word;"
for so shall succeeding readers gain wisdom by
thy notices.

CHAP. V.

The Idleness of Riding and Driving.

OF riding there be two grand kinds: first, to ride
on an animal; second, to ride on a vehicle: whereof the first is called specifically to ride, the second
to drive.

The first differeth, firstly, according to the divers
kinds of animals ridden: for some do ride horses,
some ponies, and some donkeys; whereof the two
first only do subsist in Oxford. For horses; a
man may ride a white horse, a black horse, and a
bay horse; as also a mixture of these, as a grey
horse, a horse skewbald, a horse piebald; each of
which admitteth this further subdivision: a horse
with a long tail, a horse with a short tail, a horse
with no tail, a horse with one eye, a horse broken-

kneed, a horse that plungeth, a horse that kicketh, a horse with white hoofs, a horse broken-winded; of which last are many in Oxford. The same also of ponies. Then for the manner of riding, there is this further difference; for it is possible to walk, to amble, to trot, to canter, to gallop, to race, and to leap: which last may be done, first, with the rider on the horse; second, with the rider over the horse; third, with the rider under the horse, as in Oxford. To these let be added hunting; which differeth in three ways: for it is possible to hunt a living animal, as a fox, a hare, a donkey; and it is possible to hunt a piece of flesh that is dragged on in front by a little boy; and it is possible to hunt a steeple, which is called a steeple-chase: each of which may be done, first, having a red coat or not having a red coat; second, having a dinner party afterward or not having a dinner party afterward. For driving, it differeth according to vehicles: for some do drive phaetons, some coaches, some gigs, and some tandems, and therefore more serviceable to Pluck. Furthermore some do drive their own vehicles, some the vehicles of their friends, and some vehicles which are let. Of these, the first do avoid rough places, the second and third care not: also the third, which is he that driveth let vehicles, is of two kinds; first, he that payeth; second, he that payeth not: whereof the former admitteth a still further division into two; first, he that payeth much at the time; second, he that payeth more afterward.

Let so much have been said concerning the genus, species, and difference of riding. As for the property, it is of two kinds : for some do ride that have property, and can afford; some likewise do ride that cannot afford. For the accidents, they differ as follows : for some do break their wheels, some their noses, and some their fortunes; whereof the first is separable, but the second and third inseparable : for the wheel cometh off, being broken, and so is replaced by a new wheel; but this happeneth not to the nose, nor to the fortune: whence many do leave Oxford with broken noses, but more with broken fortunes.

CHAP. VI.

The Idleness of Billiards.

THE Idleness of Billiards is an idleness good for Pluck, and not to be disesteemed, albeit many that pass do also play at billiards. Of billiard rooms useful to Pluck there be eleven, whereof one hath of late been decorated with a new painted board at the outside. There is also another in New College-lane much to be recommended, which was among the first to have metallic tables, whereby were Plucks increased not a little that year.

CHAP. VII.

The Idleness of Rowing.

ROWING, by which is understood the pushing of a boat with oars, hath not idleness in its own nature simply, for indeed sometimes he that abstaineth from rowing is idle, for the reason that he abstaineth, as with a London boatman. Yet when it be practised in the extreme, where it is not necessary, it is an idleness nevertheless; as to row every evening in an eight oar, when one hath skiffed beyond Iffley of a morning. King and Davis have good boats, also Franklin, and Mrs. Hall of ancient memory. The last mentioned hath a new sailing boat surnamed Pilot, which by reason of its goodness hath already brought in five Plucks, whereof were three in Great-go.

CHAP. VIII.

The Idleness of Music.

ALBEIT to have a good ear bringeth not a Pluck of necessity, yet the playing of many instruments leadeth to Pluck not a little, and therefore is a thing to be practised. Of instruments, the flute bringeth fewest Plucks, and the piano-forte most: for the first cannot be played for many hours in a day, but the last admitteth of this.

CHAP. IX.

The Idleness of Wine Drinking.

WINE drinking produceth Pluck each year in the
proportion following: Sherry 72, Claret 23, Ma-
deira 27, Champagne 13, Port 90. The reason
whereof is, that Port is most drunk, Champagne
least, and the rest in proportion. Of late also
hath Beer contributed not a little to produce
Plucks, for indeed Beer is a good thing for making
the mind heavy and loaded. Nevertheless as yet
beer hath not such consequence in Oxford as in
Cambridge, being a new fashion in this place.
Here let the reader consult the Synopsis of
Drinking; which, from ascertained data, has with
great care been compiled.

CHAP. X.

Concerning other Idlenesses.

THERE be many other Idlenesses of the like sort
with those mentioned : such are the kicking up of
rows in Quad, the sleeping all day in an easy
chair as does Mr. S****, the writing of poesy,
the going to plays at Abingdon, the shying at
lamps, the playing at whist with the oak sported,
the shooting with a bow and arrow, boxing, and
such like; all which, so they be taken in dis-

cretion, that is to say, as not to interrupt one
another, do lead to Pluck. But it mattereth not
to say more of them for the present, seeing that
the principle of them may be drawn from what
hath been aforesaid concerning the rest. Moreover, in Oxford they do grow up naturally, and
therefore are best to be learned by practice, and
the close following of the many good examples
thereto. Yet is there one other idleness that deserveth mention particular in this place, for that
it is not known as an idleness, albeit it is one;
that is to say, the idleness of thinking upon one's
debts, wherein is much time consumed. Therefore mind that thy debts be many, for so shalt
thou, by thinking on them more and more, come
to be better plucked: moreover thou doest good
to thy fellow creatures thereby; for what thing is
more divine than confidence betwixt man and
man? the which thou promotest exceedingly by
living upon trust.

CHAP. XI.

The things to be avoided so as to get Plucked.

AMONG things to be avoided for Pluck are these,
for in this also consisteth an idleness, yet not particular but general. As, for example, if thou really
studiest to get plucked, thou must consider that
economy of time, together with good counsel and

discreet doings, are vain things not to be practised. Thou must shun a sober friend. Thou must despise honourable ambition, having opinion of thy superiors as persons of no respect. Beware also of having a Dictionary or Lexicon in thy room; and take heed that thou attend not lecture, whether public or private. But instead of that, give thyself up to whatever thy fancy pleaseth best, disregarding all else. So much for things to be avoided, which concludeth this part of the treatise.

BOOK III.

CHAP. I.

How to demean oneself at Examination.

As to the demeaning of oneself at Examination, which was the second grand division, it consisteth of five things. For in examination are three things to be considered: first, the person who examineth; second, the person examined; third, the subject whereon the examination fixeth: whereof to the examiner belongeth question; to the person examined, answer. First, then, to consider him who examineth.

CHAP. II.

Concerning the Examiner.

LET an Examiner be defined to be one who plucketh, whence cometh it that examiners are of three kinds: first, the morose examiner, who plucketh ill-naturedly; second, the good humoured examiner, who plucketh with a smile on his face; third, the good natured examiner, who plucketh with pity. Whereof there is this difference: that the first endeavoureth to pluck; the second careth not; the third avoideth. Whence

cometh, further, a distinction of manner: for the
first questioneth oft and loud on a thing which he
knoweth to be difficult, making an austere face,
and frightening; the second speaketh blandly, and
joketh not a little, playing his wit as occasion
serveth; but the third, which is the best, desireth
thee first to sit down; then, speaking with sweet-
ness indescribable, giveth such questions as may
draw out not thy ignorance, but thy knowledge.
So the first treateth thee as a naughty school-
boy; the second, as a gentleman; but the third,
as a friend.

CHAP. III.

Concerning the Person Examined.

As for the Persons Examined, they be each of
them different, according to their different idlenesses.   For all are idle, inasmuch as they who
sport now, do sport for present idleness; and they
who read now, do read for the most part that they
may be idle afterward with better grace.   Thus
the one set are idle in practice, and the other in
expectation.   Now the different idlenesses are
seen from what hath been before writ concerning
them, therefore needless it is to mention them
afresh.   Yet let it not be omitted, that oftentimes
the person examined changeth according to the
examiner: for, first, if the examiner be morose, the

person examined becometh nervous and afraid, so
that oftentimes he forgetteth himself, and cometh
to be plucked; yea, even though he may have
taken much pains contrariwise. Second, if the examiner be good humoured, yet not good natured,
and so playeth his wit with laughing and jesting,
then doth the person examined grow flippant and
saucy, fancying he shall pass to be sure with such
a good sort of man. Third, if the examiner be a
person kind, yet having respect for himself, (as in
truth be the Oxford examiners for the most,) then
the person examined settleth into his natural self,
and so is it easily discerned whether he have ignorance or not.

CHAP. IV.

Concerning the Subject.

As for the Subject, it consisteth of Logic, Euclid,
and such other authors as have been mentioned in
the first book; besides which, is nothing else to
be observed.

CHAP. V.

The Doctrine of Questions.

FOR Questions, they differ in many ways, and are
to be considered, first, in respect of substance;
that is to say, whether they be easy or difficult:
second, in respect of quality; that is to say,

whether they be put in a loud or soft voice : third, in respect of quantity; that is to say, whether they be many or few.

Now as to substance : the morose examiner putteth an easy question in a difficult way; the good humoured examiner putteth each in its own way; the good natured examiner putteth a difficult question in an easy way.

As to quality : the morose examiner useth a loud surly voice; the good humoured examiner useth a quick voice; the good natured examiner useth a soft voice.

As to quantity : the morose examiner putteth many questions and difficult; the good humoured examiner putteth few questions and difficult; the good natured examiner putteth few questions and easy.   So to proceed to the doctrine of answers.

CHAP. VI.

The Doctrine of Answers.

OF Answers, there be three kinds useful to Pluck: the answer indirect, the answer equivocal, the answer per accidens :[e] whereof the two first do agree as genus and species.   To these three hath one other of late been added by Philosophers;

---

[e] Called also *taking a shy*, which is here used in the second intention; for verily in the common use of language, shys are taken only at Proctors, the windows of tutors, lamps, and the like.

that is to say, the answer impudent: which verily,
if well managed, doth contribute not a little in the
production of Pluck, yet by itself availeth not;
wherefore it is practised but seldom.

Of the answer indirect take the example following: for in this last examination, a certain gentleman being asked, in what year was the flood? answered, that "the flood covered the highest moun-
tains:" but being asked again the same question,
he replied thereto, that "the flood of Deucalion
is not supposed to have prevailed except over
Greece:" whereon the examiner asked yet a third
time the same question, and received for answer,
that "many shells are yet to be found in proof of
the flood."

Of the answer equivocal take the following example: a person was asked, of what substance
were the walls of Platæa? whereto he answered,
that "one side was of the same substance with the
other side:" but being asked again, he said that
"the substance at the top differed not from the
substance at the bottom."

Of the answer per accidens, as followeth: to
the question, where is Sicily? cometh answer, "in
the Deserts of Siberia, near the Cape of Good
Hope:" to the question, who were the Pelasgi?
cometh answer, that "the Pelasgi were two crows,
which settled one at Dodona, the other at Ephesus:" to the question, which party conquered at
Philippi? cometh answer, "Numa Pompilius."

Of the answer impudent, there is but one example of note : for a person being asked, in what way the pyramids were built, according to Herodotus ? answered thereto, that "he was a gentleman, and not a bricklayer."

Thus much for the examiner, the person examined, the subject, the question, and the answer : whence it is to be seen clearly, that, as respecteth demeanour at examination, it is best for Pluck that the examiner be morose; that the person examined be nervous, idle, and impudent; that the subject be such as he comprehendeth not; that the questions be many and difficult; and that the answers be *per accidens.*

CHAP. VII.

Distinctions of Little-go and Great-go.

Now all this, together with the two former books, hath been said of Great-go indeed particularly, yet also of Little-go, the appurtenances of which Great-go compriseth, as was before said. Yet since there be some things wherein these two do differ, it followeth to detail these things in order, that so the apprehension of the whole art may be full and perfect. Thus, first, Little-go admitteth not of divinity, which Great-go admitteth of, nay requireth ; second, Little-go cometh always before Great-go, but Great-go never cometh before

Little-go; third, Little-go adhereth rather to strictness of rule, but Great-go to philosophy of things; fourth, Little-go requireth not examiners of a first class, which Great-go requireth; fifth, Little-go in comparison with Great-go admitteth but little of paper work; sixth, Little-go admitteth not sciences nor writing of Greek; seventh, Little-go hath no classes, which Great-go hath.

CHAP. VIII.

Examples of approved Plucks.

AND now that these distinctions of Little-go and Great-go have been fully set forth, it remaineth, firstly, to give some examples of approved Plucks for imitation, taken from the records of Oxford and Cambridge; secondly, to lay down certain topics, whereby to argue that a man will be plucked or not; and, thirdly, to make a classification of Plucks, according to the matter: whereof the second especially is much needed for helps to betting.

Examples of approved Plucks are the following.

The case of Geoffrey C*****, who verily at Eton was counted no small genius, being able to write forty good lines of Latin poesy in the hour; yet when he came to*****, taking much pains he forgot all at last, and so was plucked.

The case of Thomas T****, who went up for

Little-go, knowing his books well, yet returned
not in triumph, for that out of spite to the examiner, as he declared, he answered every question
wrongways.

The case of John D****, commonly called
Jack o'Dandy, who because that his brothers had
been plucked, arguing it unlikely that he also
should come to be plucked, gave himself up to
racing and hunting; yet was he cut short: for
being asked, in Little-go, where Athens was? he
answered, "in the Hebrides;" nevertheless, after
two Plucks, he passed through Little-go in triumph, and so in due time he came to Great-go,
which also he passed in triumph after three
Plucks; whereon he gave a supper yet remembered and to be remembered.

The case of John F****, who indeed had read
not a little, and thereby being certain of a pass,
nevertheless was plucked. For truly many friends
offering to bet with him that he would pass, he
took their bets, with the cunning intent of demeaning himself ill; for his debts were many,
especially to Mr. P***** for horses. Thereupon
when his examination came, he did his best to
be plucked, and so succeeded, pocketing thereby
many hundreds.

The case of Paul P****, who on the morning of
his examination did eat eleven sausages, one cold
chicken, five slices of ham, three eggs, yea and
toast with bread and butter besides, in quantity

nqt to be conceived; whereby he thought to make himself courageous, yet was mistaken, for he gained nought thereby save a Pluck and a head-ache. Nevertheless he passed next time, although he was fat exceedingly, whence had a wit said of him, that he was too fat to squeeze through. Yet are wits sometimes wrong, as in this case, the reason whereof is, that they do for the most part choose what is funny, rather than what is true.

The case of Joseph J******, who being in love, meditated thereon till his Great-go came, wherein being plucked he cleared twenty thousand pounds. For indeed, when he got home, he wisely told the lady that to be plucked was the greatest honour in Oxford: whereby gaining admiration, he came to be married next week. So he quitted College, yet first paid a visit to the examiner with many thanks.

The case of Andrew B***, who having put up his name, thinking himself ready for Little-go, was told by his tutor afterward, that he was sure to come to a Pluck; yet scorned he to take his name down, and therefore was plucked with no small glory.

The case of Henry ****, in this last examina-tion, who, when he was examined, answering each question with a pun, was not understood; so when he came to be plucked, the examiner said of him to a friend in secret, (which was afterward told, as is common at Oxford, in public,) that he was witty, but not wise; thereby meaning that he would have passed but for his puns which he made.

The case of a gentleman whose name shall not be mentioned in this place, who indeed laughed exceedingly at another for being plucked, yet in the end was plucked himself, for that he could not write Latin.

The case of Abel P***, who was plucked in Little-go, and afterward added thereto so many other honours, that none were left for those that followed.

So much for instances of approved Plucks, whereon it seemeth fit to notice, that sometimes one ignorance only, as of Euclid, leadeth to Pluck, as also one idleness only, as of smoking. Yet to him who aimeth at Pluck, it is best to make sure of it by many idlenesses and many ignorances, whereby his Pluck will be more certain before examination, and more perfect afterward.

CHAP. IX.

Topics concerning Pluck.

For arguing that a man will be plucked, take the Topics following; which are writ according to the manner indeed of Aristotle, but with allowance for modern times. Now among men likely to be plucked are these, for the most part:

He that hath no friends, he that hath many

friends :ᵍ the first, because he hath none to put
him in the way to escape Pluck; the second, because he hath many to draw him therefrom.   He
that liketh good eating.   He that liketh good
drinking.   He that goeth to Ascot races.   He that
buyeth many cigars : for he that buyeth many,
smoketh many; and he that smoketh many, wasteth
much time in smoke ; and he that wasteth much
time in smoke is idle, and he that is idle is likely
to be plucked.   He that loungeth in Quad.   He
that is often proctorized.   He that hath much
money ; he that hath no money : for the first hath
too many pleasures ; and the last too little time,
since he must needs spend time in getting money.
He that readeth many books.   He that readeth
few books.   He that readeth no books.   He that
readeth novels : for verily pleasant things are
novels, and entice the mind away exceedingly.
He that sporteth not his oak.   He that taketh no
exercise : as was the case with Mr. Benjamin
B*****; who indeed did read sixteen hours a day
for three years, yet did never pass, for that he
fainted thrice in the Schools.   He that sporteth
many new whips.   He that mixeth punch well : for
truly is punch well mixed, sweet to the taste of all,
but most to the mixer.   He that keepeth more
than one large dog.   He that drinketh out of a
fox's head.   He that hath a large bill at the pastrycook's : for such an one liketh good eating ; which

ᵍ Vide Aristot. Rhet. lib. ii. cap. 23.

was before shown to produce Pluck. He that
hath many large bills : for such an one hath doubtless one large bill at the pastrycook's. He that
hath many little bills : for such an one hath doubtless one large bill. He that is in love. He that
hath been in love : for he is likely so to be again.
He that knoweth many pretty girls. He that
knoweth one pretty girl. He that roweth overmuch in eight-oared boats. He that hateth Greek.
He that was often flogged at school. He that
was never flogged at school. He that is his own
master. He that writeth not his own essays, but
employeth a barber. He that thinketh himself
clever. He that thinketh himself a fool. He that
despiseth the tutor's lectures : for such an one
thinketh himself clever. He that prideth himself
on his coat. He that prideth himself on his
waistcoat : for the same prideth himself also on
his coat. He that prideth himself on his trowsers :
for the same prideth himself on his waistcoat also.
He that is careless in little things. He that is
careless in great things. He that is over-careful
in trifles. He that hath his common books finely
bound : for such an one careth only for their outside; moreover he is fearful of soiling them with
over use. He that hath in his rooms an easy
chair wherein he constantly sitteth. He that hath
a private tutor from the first : for needs must such
an one learn to depend not on himself. He that
cometh from a large school : for needs must such

an one have many friends. He that cutteth chapel
often. He that getteth up his Greek Testament
in chapel. He that scribbleth in chapel. He that
being poor sporteth Champagne. He that betteth
and loseth many times. He that hath gone a
second time to a dog fight. He that playeth
oftentimes at billiards, yet playeth not well after
all. He that learneth boxing. He that is of a
nervous nature. He that is a radical, albeit his
father is a tory: for such an one thinketh himself
clever. He that useth a high-priced walking stick.
He that weareth his hat cocked. He that weareth
white kid gloves when shooting: for such an one
is over careful in trifles, and therefore careth not
for things important. He that belongeth not to
the Debating Society: for such an one hath no in-
terest for present history: how then for ancient,
that is, for Latin and Greek? He that driveth
tandems. He that writeth poesy. He that hunt-
eth more than twice a week. He that doeth what
his acquaintance please. He that hath more than
seven pairs of top boots. He that always weareth
a tattered cap and gown. He that getteth tipsy of
a morning. He that breaketh lamps in the street.
He that learneth more than two instruments of
music. He that eateth much pudding. He that
hath an over-pity for others that are plucked: for
verily he pitieth others because he feareth for
himself.[h] He that eateth much on the morning

[h] Vide Aristotle's Analysis of Pity.

before examination. He that rideth often, yet not well. He that rideth steeple-chases often. He that hath many German pipes. He that hath a lock of hair in his desk. He that feareth shame overmuch. He that disregardeth shame. He that thinketh he will be plucked. He that thinketh he will not be plucked. Now if thou knowest a man to be in one of these predicaments, thou mayest suppose him likely to be plucked; if thou knowest a man to be in two or three, thou mayest guess he will be plucked; but if thou knowest a man to be in sixteen or seventeen, thou mayest bet in safety, since he will be plucked for a certainty.

Thus much for Little-go and Great-go together. Then for Great-go, they likely to be plucked in Great-go are these following:—He that was plucked in Little-go. He that made a shave in Little-go. He that passed Little-go with ease: for he will take no pains towards his Great-go. He that gave a party after passing Little-go: for verily such an one esteemed his Little-go difficult, much more therefore his Great-go. He that gave a party after being plucked in Little-go: for such an one had no shame. He that was idle just before Little-go. He that took off his name at Little-go. He that was nervous in Little-go: for truly much more nervous will he be in Great-go. He that was flippant in Little-go. He that in Little-go wrote two pieces of Latin.

CHAP. X.

A Classification of Plucks according to the matter.

THESE be they likely to be Plucked, whereby a man may judge almost for a certainty if he wish to bet on a friend. For the classification of Plucks according to the matter, they are to be put in the same gradations with Passes ; for a first class in Pluck is got by him that hath the highest ignorance, as in Passes by him that hath the lowest knowledge. So also of seconds, thirds, and fourths, all which do follow in regular proportion, and therefore need not further account of them in this place. Let every man therefore try for a first, for so shall he make sure at the least of his second or third; to which honours there is but this drawback only, that they are not registered in the books, nor advertised in newspapers. Yet it is to be hoped that in the gradual progression of ignorance, this also will be brought about by the worthy reformers of these times.

CHAP. XI.

Conclusion.

SUCH is a classification of Plucks according to the matter. And so to conclude, let me say that this Treatise is now finished, wherein I take to

myself no small glory, as having been the inventor
of a new art never before known.   Yet am I not
ignorant that as it is new, so it must needs be
imperfect in part; which imperfections let future
editors mend, as occasion shall call.   For that this
art being once begun will progress no further, is a
thing not to be conceived, when is brought to
mind its great use in helping men to be plucked
on principle, which before was done at random.
So that henceforth when a man is plucked, no
person can say it was by accident or mistake of
his, seeing that all the ways leading to Pluck have
been here put down in strict order of philosophy.
Wherefore from this time when a man hath gained
a Pluck, after much pains-taking to that end, let
no person be so unjust as to take away from him
the credit thereof, and give it to others; nay,
rather let every one say, that he deserved what
he got for his labour.   And so I wish my reader
farewell; hoping from what I have writ, he may
understand fully the true way to get plucked, and
so act accordingly.

FRAGMENTS

EXAMINATION PAPERS.

TO THE READER.

LEARNED reader, as the perfection of an art consisteth in the excellence of its theory, so the excellence of an artificer consisteth in the perfection of his practice. For it is a small thing to know how to get plucked, unless thou gettest plucked also, and that both many times, and thoroughly, and with ease.

For this purpose I present thee in this book with some Pluck Examination Papers, whereby thou shalt be able to urn thy science in pluck to account ; and procure for thyself at the least a second class in pluck, if not a first, which is to be preferred. As respecteth the plan of the book, it resembleth all other examination papers of Oxford and Cambridge, like to them pointing out the degree of ignorance that is required for the gaining of honours. It behoveth thee, however, to bear in mind, that this book of papers containeth rather a collection of the most needful papers from many sets, than one entire set. Thou wilt also observe, tha sciences be introduced in these papers, somewhat beyond what is absolutely needful for being plucked ; yet did it seem to me best, rather to run hazard of being too comprehensive than too meagre. Concerning the authors here referred to, I leave thee to discover of thyself respecting them, not choosing to lay open the secrets of examinations. Nevertheless, if thou wilt come and be my pupil in the art, I promise not but I will explain to thee even these secrets ; and thus get thee plucked much more easily than will even thy present private tutor.

To conclude, I beg thee to understand these things in the way they be meant, not following the evil practice of some persons, who are wont to understand of an author, that he meaneth to ridicule things sacred or grave, because his book toucheth thereon of necessity sometimes, and who do thus distort his meaning, looking not to the context. Such persons, it seemeth to me, do forget that, from the nature of things human, every book, like a glass, changeth its feature according to the feature of him that is looking therein; or rather, indeed, that every book is likened to a certain young lady of Oxford, concerning whom, as she walketh along High-street, Mr. T. saith that she is horrible, Mr. L. that she is ugly, Mr. F. that she is bad looking, Mr. A. that she is passable, Mr. G. that she is good looking; another Mr. A. that she is pretty, Mr. P. that she is handsome, Mr. F. that she is beautiful, and Mr. N. that she is lovely; not according as the truth is, but according as he chooseth from his preconceived fancy to think of the different parts. Thus one praiseth a a blue eye, but another condemneth the same. One thinketh a curl too long, but another desireth it not to be cut. Of such an error touching this book, I beg thee to beware, except in the matter of praising, for thou hast free leave to praise it as much as thou wilt: in return for which I will not cease wishing thee to be rusticated a second time, or even to be expelled, if thou so desirest.

EXAMINATION PAPERS.

To be translated into your worst Attic Greek, in the style of Thucydides, where he is describing the character of Themistocles, Lib. i. cap. 138.

FOR Mr. Flashman was a person in whom most truly was manifested a natural strength of head, wherein he was worthy of admiration beyond any other man of his college. For by this strength of head alone, and without aid of instruction, he was the best discerner of Proctors at a distance; and, in respect of things to come, could predict for certain whether a man would be rusticated or expelled for an action. Also no man better than he perceived where he could run on tick; and he knew at once, by his natural sagacity, when it was time to leave his old tradesman, and begin a new bill elsewhere. Likewise there was no steeple-chase that he went not to: yet of him it could never be said that he was spilled. And to say all in a few words, this man, by the power of his understanding, did contrive to get numberless others rusticated and plucked, but never suffered himself either the one or the other, being considered a

person of most discreet behaviour by his tutor,
albeit in real truth he was the most noisy man of
his time.

> From the Secret History of Oxford and Cambridge, as
> translated by Hobbes of Malmsbury.

*Translate the following into your worst Ionic, in
the style of Herodotus.*

In the Atlantic Ocean, and nigh upon Corn-
wall, are some islands called anciently Cassiterides,
or the tin islands, but now surnamed Silly, which
are much to be admired for their wonderful use
and excellence. For therein does tin grow in such
plenty, that the inhabitants pass a most loveable
life, being ever able to pay their debts, from
having plenty of tin. These islands were first
discovered, according to tradition, by a man of
Cambridge; who being plucked on a time, and
having likewise great debts, determined nobly to
go in search of them upon the bare report. Therefore letting himself down at night time from his
college window, while the porter slept, and being
armed with an Ainsworth's Dictionary for defence,
he descended to the Cam, and taking a skiff, went
along with the stream, through much wild and
barbarous country, as was to be expected in those
times; till in the end, after ten days' travel, he
reached the sea coast, with much danger from the

savages, which nevertheless he escaped bravely, by wielding of his Dictionary. From the coast he proceeded by land till he came opposite to a small island; which having reached by swimming, he found thereon much tin, lying in heaps of sovereigns along the shore. Likewise the trees had for leaves bank notes, whereof some were of five pound and others of ten pound, according to their age. Seeing which, he stuffed his pockets, not excepting even his fob, with the last mentioned, wisely neglecting the first. But perceiving the islanders to approach, he was forced to flee; and thus escaping to land by swimming, reached Cambridge in thirteen days: where he paid all his own debts, besides those of his friends, albeit not a few of the notes had been destroyed by the salt water. Since his time, many Undergraduates in debt have gone on the same journey, but as yet no one hath succeeded; which is much to be lamented

> A True and Faithful Account of the Cassiterides, or Tin Islands, by Herodotus Britannicus, in his History of Undergraduates.

Historical Questions.

1. Give a particular account of the earliest gown and town rows recorded in history.

2. Does history say how many caps were broken

D

in the gown and town row, when Oxford was visited by the Queen?

3. Give an account of the number of horses driven to death last term; and compare the cavalry of Macedonia with that of Oxford and Cambridge.

4. What historical associations are connected with brandy and water? Give an account of the rise and progress of drinking in the Universities.

5. We read in the history of Greece, that it was first peopled by means of migrations. Shew how the same principle still works at Oxford and Cambridge. And explain the terms "licet migrare" and "exeat," by an historical reference to the causes which in general produce these migrations from one college to another. What was the most famous migration of this sort last term?

6. Give a full account of the last steeple-chase, detailing minutely the different falls that occurred, and what parts were bruised. Draw also a map of the ground, and explain the geographical position of each rider and of his horse respectively at the close of the race.

7. How long ago is it since the wild beasts were in the town? Give a clear narrative of the row which occurred with the authorities on that occasion.

8. Give a succinct account of the origin of the Union Society, explaining the alterations in its government since its commencement.

9. Draw up a statistical account of the imposi-

tions set last term ; distinguishing between those which were written by the man himself, and those which were paid for. Explain likewise in what parts of the town those persons live who gain an honest livelihood by writing impositions for the men ; and conclude by drawing up a table of the fluctuation in prices paid for impositions during the last ten years. Compare likewise the Cambridge and Oxford system of impositions.

1. Under what class of revenue do you put the income derived from knocking in ? Compare the revenue of Oxford, in this point of view, with that of Athens in the time of Aristides.

2. Account for the invention of swallow-tailed coats, and describe accurately the rise and progress of pea-jackets.

3. Shew what may be learnt of the history of the University from the philosophy of its flash language; and explain the principle upon which it is that Cambridge men use more flash terms than Oxford men.

4. Niebuhr, from observing that caps have tassels, and that the streets of Oxford are not macadamized, comes to the conclusion that the University was originally inhabited by the Pelasgi ; which he further confirms by observing, that the inhabitants of it depart and return periodically, according to the vacations, in which we see the

migratory habits of the Pelasgi exemplified. State the force of the argument.

Translate into your worst English the following account of an event at Cambridge.

Jamque, duabus lampadibus fractis, contra eam quæ tertia stat in vico, progrediebantur, quam subito, laniariis canibus stipatus, Proctor supervenit. Is jam antea, dum in inferiore vici parte versatur, sonitus gliscentes audiverat; quibus excitus, collegâ relicto, ad tumultum cum majore copiarum parte, summa celeritate processit. Ejus adventu perculsi proximi duo fugam capessunt. Tres jamdudum vino gravati, et pugnare et fugere æque impotentes, manu statim capti sunt. Hos ad collegias suas Proctor ferri jubet. Ipse duobus canibus stipatus cæteros duos persequitur, quorum alter dux facinoris fuerat. Et ille quidem comitem arripiens "curramus" inquit; "Proctor adest. Cito pede opus est." His dictis, ambo per vicum quemdam devium versus rivum profugiunt. Proctor cum canibus insequitur. Jamque togati juvenes marginem prope rivi tetigerant, quum alter, pede lapso, in gramen humidum sternitur; alter (atque idem dux facinoris fuit) a cane arreptus, sanguineum nasum ei dat, deinde in rivum se projicit, ad ripam oppositam nando se laturus. Hîc Proctor paulisper se inhibuit, neque enim nare didicerat et Autumnus erat: duorum præterea ejus canium

alter togatum juvenem qui prolapsus erat, vix
tenebat; alter sanguineum suum nasum abstergens
vix cernere præ lachrymis potuit. Jamque dux
facinoris ad alteram prope ripam accesserat, quum
subito, Proctore scapham per marginem quærente,
canis vulneratus pudore victus in rivum salit.
Celeriter ad ripam oppositam pervenit. Illic du-
bius in noctis tenebris, ad quem locum hostis se
abripuisset, per duas horas frustra se versat, omnes
locos explorans. Re infecta ad Proctorem super
pontem redit. Proxima die Proctor concilium
collegæ sui et Proproctorum vocat. Rem cunctam,
quo ordine gesta fuerat, exponit. Tribus togatis
qui primi capti sunt quingenti versus imponuntur.
Ille qui prope rivum prolapsus erat ad rustican-
dum terminum it. Dux facinoris non punitur,
neque enim agnosci potest.

LIVIUS NOVUS, lib. viii. cap. 7.

*Translate the following into the style of Horace's
Epistles, as badly as you can, introducing the
greatest number of false quantities that you can
think of.*

> A tradesman's son, whom once I knew,
> No matter when, or where, or who,
> Bred at the desk to daily rounds
> From pounds to pence, and pence to pounds,
> Seiz'd with a sudden fit for knowledge,
> Determin'd straight to go to College;

The thing was done as soon as said,
A cap with tassel decks his head:
He buys three teacups of his scout,
One with a saucer, two without,
And by kind Alma takes his stand,
With gown on back, and stick in hand.
Friends call and ask him out to dine,
To breakfast some, and some to wine.
Saving is what he takes delight in,
He goes whenever they invite him ;
On others' wine gets wondrous merry,
And, drunk with port, still calls for sherry.
Meanwhile to pence and farthings true,
Though rich as Crœsus, or a Jew,
He quite forgets to ask his friends
To taste his own, and make amends.
" The man is stingy," flew about ;
" Stingy's the word," his friends cried out ;
And straight devised, from animosity,
To trick him into generosity !
" I've heard," says one, "you've got some port,
" Of a most truly wondrous sort ;
" Let's have a taste, I wish to try it,
" And, if you choose, would like to buy it !"
This said, he op'd the bin, and spied
Four dozen bottles side by side ;
Demands two forks, the cork to draw,
And finds the wine without a flaw !
Just at this time, (as 'twas agreed,
In case the first friend should succeed,)
Another thirsty friend drops in,
" Oh, oh," says he, " you've op'd your bin !
" Give me a glass, we'll drink at ease,
" Or else a tumbler, which you please."
He takes a chair, (of which were plenty,)
No sooner sat, the bottle's empty !
Another bottle sees the light,
Another friend appears in sight,

Walks up the staircase, kicks the door,
Drinks up his glass, and calls for more.
Our most reluctant sees his cheer
Like smoke appear and disappear;
While drinkers fresh come every minute,
And seem to take a pleasure in it.
At last, when all his wine is gone,
Himself grown drunk from looking on,
Runs into Quad, kicks up a row,
And breaks four panes, he don't know how,
For which next morning he is fated
For two terms to be rusticated;
And learns at last, in his sobriety,
How to behave with due propriety;
Nor when to tippling he is prone,
To swill his friends', but spare his own.

Historical Essay.

The origin of boat races in the University, with a detailed account of the principal victories gained in them since their commencement; tracing their influence upon the morals and studies of the place, and comparing the Athenian navy at the death of Pericles with the navy of Oxford and Cambridge.

To be translated into your worst Latin Prose, in the style of Cicero's Orations.

Mr. President, the honourable member is mistaken; for I beg leave to affirm, in the most

distinct and positive manner, that when I said of
the honourable member that he spoke an untruth,
I meant nothing whatever against his private character.   But to return to the question before the
house : if there be any gentleman here who has at
heart the interests of this society, and therefore of
the University, and therefore of the world; if
there be any gentleman here who respects virtue
and reveres antiquity; I beseech him again and
again to consider most seriously the disastrous
consequences that must inevitably result from the
admission of dogs, however small, into the reading
room.   It is very easy for honourable members to
say that dogs are admitted at the sister University; that it is a shame to keep them out in the
street, while we ourselves are sitting snug over
our newspapers; or that they will always be
barking at the door so long as they are kept out.
All this is very easy to say, Mr. President; but I
appeal to facts; I appeal to the articles and ancient
statutes of this society, in which it is expressly
stated that dogs be not admitted.   I am sure I
have no enmity against dogs, Mr. President. They
are very useful and excellent animals in their place;
but if once admitted into our reading room, be as-
sured they will overturn the inkstands; they will
tear the books to pieces; they will smear the car-
pet with mud from the streets; they will dirty the
trowsers of honourable members; and finally and
eventually will not rest, till the ancient honours of

this society are become the common property of
the scum of creation.

Speech in the Debating Society, against the admission
of dogs into the Reading Room.

*Or the following, in the style of Cicero's
philosophical works.*

The custom of sending in bills to young men at
college, is a thing plainly contrary to the usages of
morality and the principles of religion.   But what
is more than all this, it is opposed to my doctrine
of expediency, as is to be seen in the following
respects.   It curtails generosity, that noblest principle of our nature, since men sometimes do not
give champagne at parties because they cannot
afford it, and are afraid of having to pay for it
afterwards.   It condemns the human species to
innumerable petty vexations : for the sight of bills
is odious to all, especially when one has no money.
It corrupts that serenity of mind which philosophy
requires.   It has a strong tendency to destroy all
charitable feelings between a gentleman and his
tradesman.   It checks the circulation of capital,
for it prevents tradesmen from failing.   It gives
shopkeepers a facility of cheating, enabling them
to send in the same bill twice, with additions of
what one never bought.   It promotes the extinc-
tion of the gentry : for if a man pays, he loses

his money; if he does not pay, he loses his honour. Such are some few of the evil consequences which result from the too prevalent custom of sending in bills: an impropriety on the part of tradesmen which deserves strong censure from the legislative powers. It is to be confessed, indeed, that if the custom were destroyed, it would occasion the misery of some few private shopkeepers; but what is this compared with the happiness of the whole human race, more especially the higher classes of it, which, to all appearance, have the opposite principle implanted in their nature, (for here I am constrained to allow a moral sense,) as one of the first duties of morality?

From the Improved Paley.

Critical Questions.

1. Explain the use of the word Brick in the following sentences :—As fast as a brick. As slow as a brick. As idle as a brick. To read like a brick. To run like a brick. To ride like a brick. To be a brick. As hungry as a brick. An old brick. A young brick. Do you suppose this phrase to be borrowed from ancient authors? If so, what author is it who uses the corresponding Latin or Greek term in the same manner?

2. Explain the expressions "you're sold," and "a fine sell;" and shew from the Antigone what Greek word is used in the same manner.

3. Soft fades the sun; the moon is sunk to sleep;
Through heaven's blue fringe the stars serenely peep.
An azure calm floats o'er the breathing sky,
Like Memory brooding over days gone by;
And while the owls in tender notes complain,
Grim Silence holds her solitary reign.

From which of the Prize Poems are these lines taken? Explain their beauties, and give parallel passages.

4. Has any Prize Poem appeared for the last ten years, without mention of the sun, moon, or stars in it? Explain the use of these great auxiliaries to verse-making; and shew how inferior the ancients are to the moderns in the number of their suns, moons, and stars.

5. Are you acquainted with any other use of the sun and moon besides this use of helping writers of Prize Poems? Give reasons why these authors have not made an equal use of comets, especially when modern science has discovered that there are so many to spare.

6. Trace analogically the application of the word Coach, when it is said by a man, that he has "just taken such a coach to help him through his small."

1. Tres fratres Cœli navigabant roundabout Elÿ.
Omnes drownderunt qui swimmaway non potuerunt.

Shew the false quantities in these lines. Who are the *tres fratres* supposed to have been? How many were drowned, according to the last line?

At what era of Cambridge did this important event occur? and what poet is supposed to have written the lines? Give Heyne's reading of the fourth word in the second line, and shew on what ground Porson objects to it.

2. Dr. Bentley argues that Phalaris was not plucked at college. Upon what grounds? State the argument.

3. When a man is trying to remember a thing, it is common to say that "he feels it at his fingers' ends." Shew how this expression took its rise from the custom of writing problems and chronological tables on one's nails, just before going in to be examined.

4. Explain philosophically the following terms : gip; scout; no end of clever; a tough chap; a splendid man; a shady man; and any flash terms that you can call to mind.

5. Distinguish between a drag, a tandem, a buggy, a gig, a phaeton, and a coach.

6. When Cicero designates himself as Novus homo, does he not simply mean that he was a Fresh-man? Compare the two terms.

7. Explain the Cambridge expression, "What's the odds, so long as you're happy?" and compare it with the famous saying of Solon.

Translate the following into your worst English.

Oh fortunatos nimium sua si bona nôrint
Sleevatos bachelors! neque enim sub sidera nightæ

Ad bookas sweatant; nec dum Greattomia quartam
Lingua boram strikat, saveall sine candle tenentes,
Ad beddam creepunt semasleepi; nec mane prima
Scoutus adest sævus tercentum knockibus instans
Infelix·wakare caput.   Sed munera mater
Ipsa dat Alma illis, keepuntque secantque chapellam
Quandocunque volunt.   Si non velvete minaci
Ornati incedunt, non pisces ad table higham
Quâque die comedunt, ast illis cuttere semper
Quemque licet tutorem, illis lectura nec ulla,
At secura quies, et nescia pluckere vita.

1. Explain the use of sleeves, comparing ancient and modern sleeves. What substitutes did the early Romans use for pocket handkerchiefs ? Describe Cicero's pocket handkerchief, mentioning the most remarkable holes. Was it marked with his name? At which corner? In patent ink, or thread? And by which of the maids?

2. Prove to which of the Universities these ' verses apply, from the third and sixth lines.

3. Shew from internal evidence at what period of history these lines were composed. And give the history of the most remarkable dog-latin poets.

4. Porson reads shoutibus instead⁻of knockibus. Heyne has proposed bawlibus *suo periculo ;* and another very learned editor chooses for his reading kickibus.   Shew why the present reading is preferable ; and what historians tell us concerning the manner in which scouts used to wake the men in those times.

5. From what part of these verses does Virgil seem to have borrowed?

6. Translate the following into dog-english :

> Tum forte in turri, sic fama est, reading man alta
> Invigilans studiis pensum carpebat, at illum
> Startulat horrid uproar, evertitur inkstand—ibi omnis
> Effusus labor, impurus nam labitur amnis
> Ethica per Rhetoricque.————
> Qualis ubi ingentes, coacha veniente, portmantos
> Greatcoatosqne bagosque humeros onerare ministri
> Bendentis vidi, quem dura ad munia mittit
> Angelus aut Mitre, vicinave stella Gazellæ.

By what poet of what era were these verses composed ? Give a chronological history of the principal events in his life; mentioning whether he is noticed by any contemporary poet.—What reading has been proposed by Heyne instead of " portmantos," for the sake of removing the false quantity ? Is this poet in general very particular about his quantities ?—What was the name of the person so poetically termed "reading man ?" and to what fable is allusion made by the expression " sic fama est ?"—Shew how Mr. B * * * cannot be the gentleman alluded to.

Logical and Rhetorical Questions.

1. Aristoteles Novus, among other characters which he sketches in his Rhetoric, says of the freshman, as follows :

" Now the freshman differeth from the man of standing in these respects. He often weareth his cap and gown, sometimes bearing a walking-stick also. He calleth another, " Sir." He speaketh of the boys at his college. He determineth on a first class, scorning less. He attendeth lecture with reverence. He approveth not the manner of dining. He respecteth the grass-plot. He thinketh at chapel that all others be looking at him. He seemeth ashamed at his own wine-party, making excuses many. He putteth on a grave countenance in passing the Proctor. He looketh this way and that way in walking. He appeareth proud of something. He despiseth school-boys. He buyeth one cigar. He beggeth thy pardon if thou upset his skiff. He useth often the word Governor. He buyeth a large Lexicon. He thinketh it time for him to fall in love. He goeth to bed at ten. He writeth home once a fortnight. He weareth a long tassel to his cap. He payeth ready money, refusing discount as dishonourable. He telleth you concerning his uncle. He purchaseth a Calendar to see his own name therein. He toucheth the bottle with reverence. He buyeth false collars, changeth shoes for boots, sporteth straps, and of all great things considereth the University to be the greatest, whereof in his own mind himself formeth no small portion."

Explain this character by a reference to persons whom you know, and refer each point to the wrong head in the Rhetoric. .

2. Illustrate Aristotles's sketch of youth, middle age, and old age, from the above character, and from the two following sketches of the same

gentleman at two other stages of his college career.

The same person when he hath passed his Little-go.

He getteth tipsy twice a week. He cutteth chapel and lecture. He buyeth a pea, and taketh to him a swallow-tailed coat. He promoteth rows. He sporteth a blue and white shirt. He sweareth genteelly. He talketh loud against bigotry. He buyeth cigars by the box. He borroweth a pink. He ridiculeth his former self. He considereth a quantity of bills to be gentlemanly. He boasteth of cutting the Proctor. He thinketh a first class a slow thing. He liketh to be seen with one who hath been rusticated. He acteth contumeliously at collections. He knocketh in late. He scorneth tea and bread and butter. He dineth seldom in hall. He preferreth shrewdness to learning. He writeth home once a term, and then for money. He buyeth translations. He considereth ladies to be a bore. He hath a good hand at whist, but chooseth rather to play with beginners. He cutteth his reading friend, as being slow. He shieth at the tutor's window, if there be others looking on. He encourageth whiskers. He killeth hacks. He selleth his large Lexicon for ready money. He desireth to be in the army. He considereth the University that it is a mean place, and becometh not a man that knows the world, and hath spirit.

The same when a Bachelor.

He consoleth himself by thinking that he could have done better if he had pleased. He affirmeth that he hath never enjoyed himself. He keepeth a quiet pony. He considereth a fellowship to be a good thing. He payeth his pastrycook, but not his tailor. He giveth a quiet breakfast-party twice a term. He oftentimes adviseth others. He weareth continually his cap and gown. He disputeth in divinity. He angleth for pupils. He changeth whist and écarté for chess. He approveth of toast-and-water. He affirmeth of smoking that it is vulgar. He buyeth the Waverley novels second-hand. He selleth certain of his old pictures. He writeth a pamphlet on the vices of the University. He studieth Russel's Modern Europe. He mindeth not to be seen in an old coat. He talketh of the time when he was an Undergraduate. He goeth to bed at eleven. He beginneth German. He falleth in love. He getteth sweetmeats from home, and buyeth apples by the bushel for dessert. He prideth himself on neatness. He buyeth a picture of his college. He eateth greatly at supper parties. He respecteth himself as one that is experienced. He taketh upon him to order dinner. He considereth the University to be a decent place, and himself to be a decent member thereof.

3. All members of the University wear caps and gowns.
Some ladies wear caps and gowns;
Therefore some ladies are members of the University.

Prove the correctness of this syllogism; also of the following:

A man in a skiff has got sculls in the water.
Sculls contain brains;
Therefore a man in a skiff has got water in the brains.

4. Is the following a correct sorites?

All young ladies are agreeable; all agreeable things are pleasant; all pleasure is uncertain; all uncertain things are vain; all vanity is good for nothing; therefore all young ladies are good for nothing.

5. Put the following argument into a syllogistic form:

" I must say it was a great shame in the examiners to pluck such a fellow as me, especially when I have been plucked twice before by accident. And I am sure no one can say I was idle; for I read all day through the last fortnight, except on hunting days. However, I dare say the Governor wont find it out, for he's a slow brick."

6. The schoolmen define man to be " animal implume." Prove this definition to be false, from the fact that a man is capable of being plucked.

7. Are the speeches in the Union Society to be considered as deliberative, judicial, or epideictic? Explain the singular circumstance that no mention of the Union Society is to be found in Aristotle's Politics.

8. "We understand that Major D**of W***, near Yarmouth, has been convicted of receiving three kegs of smuggled brandy." May not this be called an "illicit process of the major?"

9. Explain the logical distribution of a term by reference to the meaning of the word Term-trotter.

10. Distinguish metaphysically between Oxford milk and Oxford cream, shewing from Plato how much water is necessary to constitute the first, and how much milk the last.

Translate the following into your worst English.

Οἱ δὲ ἐπειδὴ παρεσκεύαστο αὐτοῖς, τηρήσαντες νύκτα χειμερινὸν ὕδατι, καὶ ἀνέμῳ, καὶ ἅμα ἀσέληνον, ἐξῄεσαν. Ἡγεῖτο δὲ Σμῖθος ὅσπερ καὶ τῆς πείρας αἴτιος ἦν. Καὶ πρῶτον μὲν τρία βλάνκεττα συνδήσαντες ὑνγησαν αὐτὰ ἔξω. Τότε δὲ ὁ Σμιθὸς παραινέσας Θομψῶνα καὶ Ἰονσῶνα καὶ Ἰακωβσῶνα δουνλέττει ἔαυτον πρὸς τὴν γῆν. Οἱ δ' ἄλλοι ἐφόλλουσαν αὐτόν. Καὶ δὴ ὁ Θομψῶν καὶ ὁ Ἰονσὼν ἄνευ ψόφου ἐδουνγόττησαν· ὁ δὲ Ἰακωβσῶν, (ὑπέρφαττος γὰρ ἦν,) βλανκέττων τινὸς βρεακθέντος, φαλλδουνεῖ, καὶ τὸν πορτερὸν ἐξ ὕπνου ἀνεγείρει. Οἱ ἄλλοι μὲν ἐξέφυγον· ὁ δὲ πορτερὸς καὶ ὑποπορτερὸς προσελθόντες Ἰακωβσῶνα τὸν κακοδαίμονα συλλαμβάνουσι. Οἱ δὲ τρεῖς οἱ ἀποφυγόντες πολλὴν ὁδὸν ῥυννήσαντες ὡς τάχιστα, τέλος ἐστόππησαν· καὶ πολ-

λῶν γνώμων λεχθείσων ἐνίκησεν ἡ τελευταία ἡ
τοῦ Σμίθου, ὅτι δεῖ λάρκην ἔχειν, καὶ τότε λαρκή-
σαντας εἰς κολληγίαν πρὸς τὸν πορτερὸν ῥετύρνειν.
τὸ δὲ ὄνομα τοῦ πορτεροῦ ἦν Ἰωάννης, καὶ τοῦ
ὑποπορτεροῦ Θώμας. Ταῦτα οὖν δετερμινήσαντες
καὶ ἔπραξαν οὕτως. Πρῶτον γὰρ λίθοις ἐβρεάκ-
ησαν πάνας εἴκοσι ἐν τῷ στρήτῳ, κ. τ. λ.

The Secret History of Oxford, by THUCYDIDES NOVUS.

Put the following into bad English verse.

Ὣς ἔφατ'· οἱ δὲ κλάπον Μάσιχοι μάλα γηθόσυνοι κῆρ,
Καὶ τῶν ἰσσόντων γένετο ἰαχή τε καὶ ὕπρωρ.
Καὶ τότε Σίνκλαιρος Σκιμμήριος ἆλτο χαμᾶζε·
Πολλὰς ἔχων πατέρας, καὶ σῶμ' Αἴαντι ἐοικώς.
Τὸν Λοΐδην δὲ κάκ' ὀσσόμενος προσέφη τε καὶ εἶπεν·
" Τίπτε μέλει ὑμῖν, Μάσιχοι, ὅτι Ῥάμβλερός εἰμι;
Καὶ τί πότ' ἐστ' ὑμῖν αὐθάριτί με πρηφέντειν;
Ἀλλ' ὅδ' ἀνὴρ Μασίχης περὶ πάντων ἔμμεναι ἄλλων,
Πάντων δὲ ῥυλεῖν ἐθέλει, καὶ πάντας ἀβύζειν,
Πᾶσι δὲ κομμανδεῖν· ἅτιν' οὐ πείσεσθαι ὀΐω.
Εἰ δέ μιν εὐσηηκοντ' ἔθεσαν θεοὶ αἰὲν ἐόντες
Τοὔνεκά οἱ προθέουσιν ὀνείδεα πᾶσι λέγεσθαι;
Πάντας γ' ἐξπέλλειν ἀγαθοὺς τρείουσι Μασεῖχοι,
Οἷς αἰεί τοι ἔρις τε φίλη πόλεμοί τε μάχαι τέ·
Μήδ' οὕτως κλάσσμαν πὲρ ἐὼν, Μασίχη θέοειδες,
Κλέπτε νόῳ· ἐπεὶ οὐ ψήφῳ ἐξπέλλεαι ἡμᾶς."

UNIOMACHIA.

1. To what alteration in the constitution of the
Union do these verses allude?

2. What is understood by the disputed term
Ῥάμβλερος? Do you agree with the learned

editor in supposing it must have meant some opposition society, which has been gradually destroyed in the progress of college generations?

3. Who was the hero Μασίχης, and what do we know of his history? Discuss this.

4. Dunderheadius explains Σίνκλαιρος, by a reference to the Saxon language. Give any explanation of your own that you think better.

5. Explain the term εὐσππηκοντ', mentioning who is the best speaker in the Union at present, and of what country he is. Also what the last motion was that he introduced, and whether it passed or not.

Essay in Moral Philosophy.

1. Connect Plato's theory with New College puddings, and discuss the latter subject.

2. Defend upon philosophical principles the conduct of the Philosopher, in having a large and small hole cut in his door for his cat and kitten. What was the colour of this famous cat?

3. Discuss the theory which justifies men in taking freshmen's caps and gowns instead of their own academicals, when at a party.

4. Make clear the correctness of the following reasons for cutting a man, according to Aristotle's doctrine of friendship in the Ethics :

" A man may be cut, because he has got on an old coat. Because he has got on a white hat in winter. Because he has taken to reading. Because he has gained a scholarship. Because he advised you. Because you have found a new acquaintance. Because he would not go with you to Abingdon in a tandem. Because he would not get tipsy at your request. Because he has taken to wearing his cap and gown. Because he refused to meet C * * * at a wine party. Because his wine is bad. Because his rooms are up three pair of stairs, and therefore difficult to be got at. Because another man says he is an ass. · Because he would not go with you on the river. Because his hat is narrow brimmed. Because you find it a bore to nod. Because his dog hurt yours.

Mathematical Questions.

1. A Freshman engages to· eat a sponge-cake while a Bachelor is drinking a bottle of port. The Bachelor begins half a second before the Freshman, and has reached his ninth glass by the time that the Freshman is swallowing the sixth mouthful. How long will it be before the Freshman is choked?

2. A and B had drunk some port at the proportionate rate of three bottles to five. A bets B, after this, that he shall be able to distinguish be-

tween port and sherry after sipping six times of each alternately. He is blindfolded accordingly, and ceases to distinguish when he has sipped half as many times as B had drunk more glasses than himself. How many glasses had A drunk before he began sipping?

3. At what ratio of velocity will an empty bottle in concussion with a nose break the nose in question? Explain this mathematical process of reduction to vulgar fractions.

4. Allowing every man in the University to have six friends, each of whom has six friends, and so on; at what degree of acquaintanceship is every man connected with every man, supposing there to be 1200 men?

5. If one bottle is enough for eight reading men and a half, how many bottles will be requisite for one man who does not read?

6. Of two Cambridge controversialists, one asserts that the apple which Newton saw fall was a codling, the other that it was a golden pippin. State the dispute of these learned philosophers, and shew its effect upon Newton's theory.

7. According to the theory of light, what light is best for escaping the eye of the Proctor?

8. If three men out of seven are plucked when the examiner is in a good humour, how many out of nine will be plucked when he is in a bad humour?

9. Let A be a hunter, B a freshman on the

hunter's back, C a fence, and D a muddy ditch on the other side of the fence. The hunter A suddenly draws up at the fence C. What connection will follow between the freshman B and the ditch D?

THE END.

VINCENT, PRINTER, OXFORD.

BOOKS LATELY PUBLISHED
BY J. VINCENT, OXFORD.

HINTS TO STUDENTS in reading for CLASSICAL
HONOURS, in the University of Oxford. Second edition,
revised. By a CLASS MAN. 12mo. price 1s.

JOHANNIS GILPINI ITER, LATINE REDDI-
TUM. "Post equitem sedet atra cura."—*Hor.* Editio Altera.
foolscap 8vo. price 1s. 6d.

THE RIME OF THE NEW-MADE BACCA-
LERE, in seven parts. Second edition, foolscap 8vo. price
1s. 6d.

> And now I WILL UNCLASP A SECRET BOOK,
> And to your quick-conceiving discontents
> I'll read you *matter deep and dangerous;*
> As full of peril and advent'rous spirit
> As to o'erwalk a current, roaring loud,
> On the unsteadfast footing of a spear.
> HENRY IV. act i. sc. 3.

VIÆ PER ANGLIAM FERRO STRATÆ. Editio
Altera. Price 1s.

> But times are altered, trade's unfeeling train
> Usurp the land, and dispossess the swain.
> GOLDSMITH'S DESERTED VILLAGE.

A LEGEND OF THE LATE ILLUMINATION.
Latin and English, foolscap 8vo. price 6d.

A LOVING AND LOYAL BALLAD, on the Oc-
casion of the Happy Delivery of her Most Gracious Majesty.
foolscap 8vo. price 6d.

POEMA CANINO-ANGLICO-LATINUM, super
Adventu Recenti Serenissimarum Principum, non Cancellarii
Præmio donatum aut donandum, nec in Theatro Sheldoniano
recitatum aut recitandum. post 8vo. price 1s.

> Hic meret æra liber Sosiis.
> HORAT.

Milton Keynes UK
Ingram Content Group UK Ltd.
UKHW051851300624
444825UK00004B/148

9 783385 123731